JUST NORMAN

DAPHNE R. FOSTER

Illustrations by Jackie Crofts

AuthorHouse™ UK Ltd.
1663 Liberty Drive
Bloomington, IN 47403 USA
www.authorhouse.co.uk
Phone: 0800.197.4150

Published by AuthorHouse 02/19/2014

ISBN: 978-1-4918-8421-8 (sc)
ISBN: 978-1-4918-9018-9 (e)

Library of Congress Control Number: 2014900746

This book is printed on acid-free paper.

Because of the dynamic nature of the Internet, any web addresses or links contained in this book may have changed since publication and may no longer be valid. The views expressed in this work are solely those of the author and do not necessarily reflect the views of the publisher, and the publisher hereby disclaims any responsibility for them.

authorHOUSE®

Duck ....Norman

Cats .... Charlie and Cindy

Mice .... Maurice and Mindy

Rabbits .... Roland and Rosie

Duck sleeps in chicken house
Cats sleep in the house
Mice sleep in the corner of
the barn in the loft
Rabbits in a burrow under
the chicken house
Pond in the farmyard

Table of Contents

THE RABBIT BURROW

Brrrr! It feels cold this morning - it feels like Autumn could almost be here. I must get up, I do hope the girls (chickens) don't make too much fuss. They can be very pecky if I make too much noise, so I try to be as quiet as I can, that is when I go out of the chicken house, and I move as quickly as I can.

Hooray! Not one peck! Now for my morning swim. Wheee! Lovely, lovely, lovely! The water is great. The sun is coming up and I feel that this is going to be a good day.

'Morning, Charlie and Cindy, you're out and about early!' (these are the farm cats)

'Yes,' replied Charlie, 'the hoover is going full pelt in there', pointing towards the farmhouse, 'you can't hear yourself think in there, so we are off to do a bit of sunbathing, we have a good spot near the side of the barn. See you later.'

'By the way, my name is Norman, I forgot to tell you that. I am a white duck and there are no other ducks here at present, but who knows what may happen later!'

Just under the chicken house there is a rabbit burrow where my friends Roland and Rosie live. They are safe there away from the foxes and any other predators. They only moved there nine months ago when their previous home was dug up when a new housing estate was started the other side of the village. We all look after one another here and help each other out when we can, as you will see as the story goes on.

The other friends I haven't yet mentioned are Maurice and Mindy, and they are two mice who live in the barn in a corner of the hayloft, (a bit precarious, but they seem to like it up there).

Well, what to do now that I am nice and fresh from my swim - although I will go back again later for some fun in the water. Let's see what breakfast has to offer, maybe there is some breakfast left for me though I'll have to be quick or everyone else will have eaten it up. Yippeee! First in the queue today, fresh corn today, I'm hungry! Look out, here come the rest of the farmyard contents! I must go, mustn't be too greedy! I think I'm going to find some sun, have a clean-up, then forty winks, hey ho! Whaaaaaaaat was that! Hey, who is making all that noise? I was having my shut eye, no chance now! It was Dan the dog and he sounded excited. Can't a chap have a nod off now?

I had better go and see what all the fuss is about. Oh no! He has found Roland and Rosie's house, it is the burrow under the chicken shed that I told you about earlier. I must create a diversion so that they can get away safely, but I need Charlie and Cindy's help. 'Hey, you two, come and help me, quickly please', Dan has found Roland's house and they need someone to get Dan's attention whilst they get away. 'Ooookay, we'll come, we like to tease Dan a bit now and then.' They all arrived near the chicken shed. The girls (chickens) were also in a state, clucking and flapping about. The cats ran up to Dan and started to catch his tail with their claws. 'Hey leave me alone! I've found the rabbit hole that I have been looking for for ages.'

'Don't do any more digging to it,' said the cats. The dog had done quite a bit of digging and was getting near to the main part of the burrow. 'Why, I'm having some fun! I'd like to see someone mess your kennel about, you wouldn't think that was funny, would you?'

'No, but these are only rabbits.'

'Only rabbits? Well, I never thought I would hear you say such a thing! They are our friends and we must all stick together if we want to survive in this farmyard. So leave them alone, or we will not be your friend and everyone needs friends.'

The dog was reluctant to leave the hole, but he agreed that, yes, he liked all of his friends and he would try and be a bit more thoughtful in the future. Wheeeew! That was a close shave for the rabbits.

I feel quite tired after that! Maybe, just maybe I can continue my forty winks now.

Hey Ho! Zzzzzzzzzz ......

Well, the rest of the day proved to be quite quiet and well before the sun went down I went to the chicken house to go to bed. Ooooh, I hope I can get in without too much fuss (and pecks). I'll make straight for my bed, but no, as I went through the door there was a greeting such as I had never had before. The girls had heard what I had done that day (remember the dog digging) and they all clucked in unison and said what a clever duck I was to fetch the cats so quickly and thus save the house for Roland and Rosie. I said 'It was nothing!' I hoped someone one day would help me too if I was in trouble, but that could be another story!

THE POND

Hi - it's me again, Norman the duck. Let me see, yes, last week I went for a walk after breakfast. I had been told about a nice little pond in the High Street, it was a fair way to go, but I thought, well, I've got time and it's a nice day, what the heck! So off I went.

Who would have thought that it would turn out the way it did and it was like thisssssssssss ......

Passing the field next to the farm was a herd of cows. They were too busy to notice me wandering along the lane. Suddenly, round the corner of the lane came this tractor, well, noise or what! It was getting on a bit, the tractor I mean, and it wheezed along like an old tin can, wobbling all over the place. I made a jump for the ditch and made it just in time! He coughed and said 'Sorry mate, I'm late and he wants me to go faster, but I've got a bit of a flat back tyre. He hasn't noticed it yet, so it's making me wobble far more than I usually do. I'm looking forward to a good rest when I get back. The ploughing is nearly finished now, thank goodness!' With that he trundled off towards the farmyard and his beloved barn for a rest (the same barn where Maurice and Mindy the mice lived).

Well, after the tractor had gone off down the lane I scrambled out of the ditch looking not like a white duck at all! There was some muddy water at the bottom, so I had streaks of mud and green grass stains all over my feathers, yuck! I couldn't wait to get to this new pond to have a good clean-up!

A horse stood at a gate in a field as I wandered on. 'Good heavens, what have we here?' he said, 'Is it a duck or an alien?'

'Ho, ho, very funny!' I replied, feeling very grubby, 'I fell into a ditch!' and I told him about the tractor.

'I've seen him too' he replied, 'poor old soul, needs a rest that one does.'

'Do you know how far it is to the pond in the High Street? It seems as though I've been walking for ages.'

'Oh that, well if you keep straight on you will come to a junction and the pond is just across the road. Mind the road as it can be busy sometimes'.

I thanked him and I waddled on at a faster pace knowing that I hadn't very far to go. True as he said, I came to the junction, and low and behold, there it was. Steady now, I told myself, watch the road! I did, and all was quiet, so I quickly went across and plunged into the water. Yippeeee! It felt so good. After I had been under a few times I felt clean once more and had a look around to see who was about. At the end of the pond amongst the reeds were two moor-hens and their baby chicks. One of the parents swam to me demanding to know what I was doing there.

'This pond belongs to everyone, but we haven't seen you here before. Where have you sprung from?'

'I live at Forty Acre Farm and I heard that there was a pond in the High Street, so I thought I would check it out. Don't worry, I'm not staying very long.'

'Good,' he replied, ' because we have six Khaki's coming back any minute (they are the brown ducks) and they won't be very pleased to see you swimming around here.'

Oh! I thought won't they, they don't own the pond and I'll tell them so or my name isn't Norman!

Whoosh, in they came, landing like so many aeroplanes, my there did seem a lot of them though! Well, here goes!

'Hi chaps', I said, addressing the males, 'just visiting, not going to stop long, just needed a bit of a clean-up.'

'That's okay mate!' they said, 'Come and meet the others.'

Phew! I thought, they are friendly, thank goodness!

'Hi everyone', I said, 'nice to meet you.'

We swapped news, me about the farm and them about where they had been, how long they had been there, etc. A mother and child came to feed them some bread, they let me have some, but I wasn't very keen, I preferred my usual meals at the farm.

As the day wore on I thought of the long journey back. Oh my, what a long way! I said so to one of the ducks and they said, 'Walk! You're a duck! Fly back!

'Fly, I said, I don't do that.'

They fell about laughing, a duck that doesn't fly! Well, I never! I hung my head, until one said, 'Come on, I'll show you.'

Well, it wasn't easy, but I gave it a shot and after a few false starts I was away, wheee! Why hadn't I done this before? It will take no time at all to get home. So, off I flew, keeping low, back to the farm. It was a very surprised dog to see me land near the pond and he began to bark. Stop that, you fool, it's only me – Norman! I've been on a visit to the High Street pond and the ducks there showed me how to fly, so that I don't always have to walk everywhere. I think it might well come in useful one day, of that I am sure, as you will no doubt find out ...

CATS AND MICE

Next day and it's Midday and the sun is still quite warm for the time of year.

Charlie and Cindy the farm cats were dozing in the sun on the roof of the old barn where Maurice and Mindy the two mice lived in the hayloft.

The two mice had had a busy morning, moving ears of corn from the floor of the barn to the loft and they were quite tired. Never the less, it was important that they stored as much as possible to see them through the winter months. They had already collected hips and haws (the berries from wild roses and hawthorn) which were safely stored and after the corn, any item that would keep had to be collected. So, on they went until it was almost dusk.

After the sun had almost gone down, the two cats strolled around the barn and Mindy spotted the two mice picking up the odd ears of corn. Now, thought Mindy, time for some fun. She crept low to the ground in the hope that she wouldn't be seen. But no she was too big not to be seen and Maurice and Mindy scuttled under a large wooden box which stood nearby. They sat still hoping that the cats would go away, but, no, they sat one each side of the box, patiently waiting for either of the mice to appear.

They didn't intend to harm them, just have a little fun. After a while, Dan the dog came along, 'What are you two doing there?' he said.

'Nooooothing,' said the cats, beginning to wash their faces.

'If I didn't know better,' said Dan, 'I would think that you have Maurice and Mindy under that box.'

'Uuus? Never!'

'Well, you won't mind me looking then, will you.'

Charlie got up and said, 'I've just remembered something that I must do. Bye for now'.

He was quickly followed by Cindy, who also remembered that she had someone to see.

After they had gone, Dan wagged his tail and said to the box 'It's okay, you can come out now, they've gone.'

Maurice and Mindy cautiously looked out and thanked Dan very much for looking out for them.

'It's okay, glad to be of some help.' said Dan.

Dan wandered off to the pond and told me (Norman) all about it. 'I will give them a piece of my mind when I see them.' I said, 'They know that Maurice and Mindy have to get their winter store in, and now they've lost some time.'

The following day I saw the two cats and they were well and truly told off, (I'm not a duck to be messed with!). Now, I told them you can go and collect some of the corn for them so that they don't lose out on their store. After having a moan and trying to slide away, they agreed and between them helped fill up Maurice and Mindy's store.

After all, as I said before, they never know when they themselves may need a helping hand.

THE ORCHARD

Well, today it's raining, yes I know - perfect weather for a duck like me! After some extra time swimming in the pond, I decided to seek out Roland and Rosie the Rabbits. They usually come out in the daytime if it's raining, as there is less chance of Dan or the cats being about. If they were, they usually chased them and it was worrying for them, even though it was only a game. No sign of dog or cats, phew!

`Hello you two, I thought I'd find you here. Where are you off to, do you mind if I tag along? I'm at a bit of a loose end today.`

'Not at all', they replied, 'we're going along to the apple orchard. There are some lovely patches of dandelions and some very sweet grass there. Rosie fancies a change from the local lot,' said Roland.

So, off we went, it was down the lane a bit, the opposite way to when I went to the High Street. I had to keep a fast waddle going as the rabbits could hop along at some speed. When we arrived the gate was shut, but the rabbits knew of a hole in the hedge and we were quickly inside the orchard. Oooh! I hadn't been here before, lots of lovely trees. A few fallen apples were lying around, they were called tacks as they had small pieces of bad in them. The birds didn't mind, a blackbird was having a lovely time with one.

'Take care,' he told us, 'there is a rumour that a fox comes this way sometimes.'

' Thanks for the warning,' I said. I took off to fly around the area to have a look. About two fields away I spied him, he was having a nap, so for the time being we were safe, but I warned the rabbits anyway.

I sat under a tree and was about to doze off when the rabbits (they have exceptional hearing) said, 'We'd better get going, someone or something is coming our way.'

Sure enough, before we could reach the hole in the hedge the fox appeared. Roland and Rosie ran as fast as they could, through the hole in the hedge and on down the lane, the fox behind chasing them.

I had taken to the air and was safe. The fox was catching the rabbits up, so I thought I must do something more to distract the him. I swooped down and picked an apple up from the end of the orchard, flew to where the fox was running and dropped the apple on his head. He was so surprised that he stopped in his tracks, allowing the rabbits to get well ahead and back to their burrow and safety.

The fox never dared to come into the farmyard because of the dog, you see.

Well, that was a close shave, I'll think twice about going to the orchard again, unless we have Dan the dog with us, of course.

HEDGEHOG

The cold weather was here and everyone was nipping about trying to keep warm or staying indoors watching the snow drifting down. The pond was not frozen over, but I didn't swim around too long - it was far too cold. A quick dip and out again!

I was feeling a bit bored, no one seemed to be about when I heard a voice say, 'Hey, what date is it? I seem to be in a bit of a muddle, it's not spring is it?'

'No, my old mucker', (a name I called anyone I didn't know, but who looked friendly) 'you're miles out! It's winter, what on earth are you doing out? You should be asleep for the winter.' It was a hedgehog, you see, and they usually wake up in the spring.

'Oh no, what am I going to do?', I can't remember where my house was and I'm going to freeeeze if I stay out very long in this weather. Oh, why oh why did I wake up?

'Don't panic, flower', I said (another pet name of mine) 'I've an idea, follow me.'

I first went to the chicken shed, where I sleep, to see if he could stay there.

'Whaaaat is that?' they clucked, 'No no no, he can't come in here! We can't have him with us, he will never get any sleep, we chatter too much.'

So off we plodded again, the hedgehog getting slower as he was getting colder. 'I know,' I said, ' Come to the big barn. I'm sure we can find you a nice quiet space in there, and it's warm!'

So, we arrived at the barn and went under the door where there was a piece of planking missing. All was quiet. In the corner were some bales of straw, but nothing that you could snuggle down in to keep warm. 'Hang on a minute, I'll just have a word with my two friends who live here.' Just then Mindy's face appeared over the edge of the loft.

'What's up Norman, can we help you? I explained about the hedgehog and they said if he could get up to the hayloft there was plenty of room for him to sleep in one of the corners up there. But, how to get him up there, if we didn't hurry he would fall asleep standing up!

In the corner, I saw an old piece of sacking. I know, I thought, if I make a loop I can put hedgehog in it and fly up to the loft. It was worth a try. Well, trying to get a sleepy hedgehog into the loop, - he kept rolling out as fast as I put him in.

This is not working until I thought again and doubled the loop, pushed and prodded him in, gathered up the ends and tried to take off.

The first two attempts were failures, but the third time I was lucky and wobbling a lot I managed to reach the hayloft and tipped him out of the loops. He would have rolled back down to the floor if the two mice hadn't stopped him, they guided him to a nice warm place and he fell asleep straight away. Thanks guys, I think I will have to stay too tonight as the snow is so thick and it has gone dark. I'll have to wait until the morning to get back to the chicken house, so I too found a nice warm corner, and oh boy, I was ready too for some shut-eye!

MEETING DONK

Zzzzzzzzzz, oh, I feel sleepy this morning! The girls (hens) kept me awake with their chatting last night, local gossip passed on to them by the garden birds, no doubt.

I'd better go to the pond and have a quick dip - it might wake me up a bit. Ooh, this feels better. No time to lose, best get my breakfast, then I'm popping to see my friends in the nearby pond in the High Street. They're expecting some visitors today.

I think I will walk part of the way as I miss so much when I fly, but then, it is safer sometimes.

'Hi to you Dobbin,' (it was the horse I'd spoken to before) he had his head over the gate.

'Hello,' he replied, 'meet my friend Donk!'

'Donk,' I said, 'what a strange name for a friend.'

'Well, he is a donkey, mate, what else would he be called?'

Donk peered at me through the middle bars of the gate as he wasn't as tall as Dobbin. 'Who are you, 'Quack', I suppose! He he he.'

'No, I am certainly not!' I replied, 'I'm Norman.'

He fell about laughing, 'Norman, a duck called Norman? Now I've heard it all!'

'Hurumph, I'm going if you are going to insult me!'

'Hang on' said Dobbin, 'he was only getting his own back, he didn't mean any harm, Norman, let's all be friends!'

'Okay,' I said, not liking not to be friends, everyone needs them. So, with a wave and a chuckle, off I went again.

As I approached the pond in the High Street, a great deal of noise was coming from the direction of the end of the pond. Oh! I thought, the guests have arrived, I wonder what they or who they are. Well, I soon found out, the strangers were four Canadian Geese, they were resting from their long flight from the North, (although I'm not sure where in the North they had flown from).

'Hi guys,' I said as I swam up to them.

'What have we here then?' said one female goose. I wagged my tail at her and she fluttered her eyelashes at me.

Steady on, I thought to myself. These chaps may not be friendly, but I needn't have worried. They said, 'Hiya mate, good to meet you.'

'Where are you actually going to, I mean where are you hoping to finally live?' I asked.

'Well, we heard on the grapevine that a farm called Forty Acres was a good place to be. It has a pond and some good fields nearby as well.'

You could have knocked me down with a feather, my farm! Now, I'm not one to be worried , but this news was not good. If these chaps arrived on the farm there would be chaos.

Everyone had their place and things ran smoothly there most of the time. I said that I knew where the farm was as I lived there. This got their attention.

'Well, you can fill us in mate, then can't you, is it far?'

I told them I could take them there, so after a little rest we took off and were soon landing in a nearby field near the farm.

'Is this it?' they said, 'not much of a farm, is it! We need a lot of green fields and a very large farm!'

'Well, my muckers, this farm won't be for you, I don't think.'

Just then Dan the dog came along on his daily patrol and scattered the geese. they hadn't banked on getting disturbed and so they took off in great haste.

Thanks, but no thanks,' they honked, 'be seeing you ...' and with that they flew off into the distance. Phew, I thought, that was a close one!

'Who was that?" asked Dan.

'Oh, only some friends who dropped in to see me. I'm off to bed, Dan. See you in the morning.'

'Yes,' said Dan, 'see you in the morning.'

THE CHILDREN'S VISIT

It was Friday, nearing the weekend and the weather was very pleasant. News was that the Farmer's wife's cousin was to visit the farm bringing three small children with them, all under the age of ten! Now, I'm not averse to children, when I am swimming in the middle of the pond, but, having them chase me, not that I think these children might, is not funny when you only have short legs and they have long ones and the pond seems a long way off. I am going to be very careful until I know what they are like. The word has spread about the visit and everyone was going about looking round corners and finding some swift getaway places for safety.

Well, the afternoon came and a car arrived with the cousin and her children, one boy and two girls. The children ran into the farm which seemed all of two minutes and then ran out into the farmyard itself , scattering the hens and making Dan the dog bark.

Oh no! I thought, it's going to be one of those visits, time to make myself scarce! I hid in a patch of stinging nettles, I should be safe here I thought. Just then I heard voices, the children were talking.

'Just because we run fast doesn't mean that we are going to frighten the animals', said one, 'it's just that we have been cooped up in the car for two hours and we just needed some fresh air.'

'Yes,' said another, 'I'm looking forward to finding out where they all are, it seems very quiet all of a sudden, where are all of the animals?'

'I expect they have a snooze this time of the day,' said the third child, 'perhaps they will come out later and we can see them all.'

The children returned to the Farmhouse for their tea and word spread that it was safe to come out. Gradually the Farmyard came to life, each one doing their usual things, cleaning, washing, eating, etc. I went off to the pond for my evening swim and I was walking back to the chicken house to get ready for bed, when I was confronted by three inquisitive faces, 'Look" they said, 'a duck, it must be the only one here, I think, he is all on his own, do you think he is lonely?'

No chance, I thought, me, lonely? You must be joking! Do you think he will let me stroke him? Whaat! Stroke me? What does he think I am, a dog? Then one of the girls said, 'You don't stroke ducks, silly, you just talk to them.'

Hey ho, someone has some sense, so I stopped still and eyed them all up.

'Do you know,' said the other girl, 'I really think he knows what we are saying, he just winked at me! Let's just follow him and see where he goes to sleep.'

The time was getting on and I was going to be shut out if I didn't hurry. So, I walked as fast as I could towards the chicken house and went inside. The girls were already settling down for the night. One said, 'You're late, you just got in by the skin of your teeth young man, don't do it again!'

I crept into my bed and settled down for the night. Outside, the children said, 'Well, fancy a duck sleeping with the chickens! Let's go and tell Mum, and I'm feeling sleepy, too.'

All three hurried back to the Farmhouse, all looking forward to the next day to see the rest of the farm animals and what adventures they could have. Hey ho, better get some rest, it looks like being another busy day tomorrow, zzzzzzzzzz .....!

DONK'S NEW SHOES

Today it's quiet in the farmyard as the children have gone to visit another relative who lived by the sea. I overheard them talking about it, they were quite excited. I thought I would visit my friends in the village who lived by the pond.

I was walking along the lane thinking and muttering, mutter, mutter, when a voice said, 'Well, old son, what are you muttering about? I could hear you from the corner of the field'. It was Dobbin, the old horse. He had his head over the field gate.

'Oh! something and nothing', I said and I told him about the visiting children.

'I know.' he replied. 'They came for a walk the other day and brought me a nice tasty carrot and a piece of apple for Donk.

'Where is Donk?' I asked, he was usually staring at me through the middle bars.

'The farrier is fitting new shoes on him today as the others were well-worn and hurt him when he walked.'

'Oh,' I said, 'that's good,' thinking to myself, thank goodness I don't have to have shoes nailed to my feet, perish the thought! I wished Dobbin a 'good morning' and went on my way.

When I reached the pond all was quiet, too quiet, where is everyone I thought. I soon found out, they were all hiding in the reeds, some children had arrived and were throwing things at the ducks and the little tiny baby moor-hens. The parents were in a state. I must try and do something to fix this, I thought. I took off and flew towards the village shop. Luckily the door was open. I skidded to a halt just inside the door. (My landing hasn't been perfected yet.)

'Whoa,' said a voice, 'what have we here?' I immediately quacked as loud as I could and went out of the door. The shopkeeper followed me, I stopped and quacked again and he said to his wife, 'Look after the shop will you? I reckon there is something up at the pond, I am going to follow the duck.'

He did just that, and as soon as he saw what the children were doing he stopped them and told them if he caught them doing it again he would go and see their parents to explain that they were being cruel to the pond dwellers.

The children hung their heads and promised to behave in the future. The ducks and moor-hens came to the side and the shopkeeper said to them, you've got your friend here to thank. He came and brought me here, he was worried for you.

'Thanks mate', said one of the drakes, 'they wouldn't stop no matter where we went, they followed us.'

'I think you will be safe from now on,' I said, 'it was a pleasure my old friend'. After we had had a good natter, I flew back home, I was too tired to walk. I was just in time for tea, then I had my evening swim, after which I headed off for my bed and some shut-eye, I wonder what tomorrow will bring?Ah! Zzzzzzzzzz

COMBINE HARVESTER

I was late getting up this morning and the chickens woke me with a start. 'Come on bonny lad, get up, the whole farm is awake and the sun is up, too.' 'Whaaat!' I said, I was still sleepy. 'Come on, get up!' they said, 'You've missed breakfast by half an hour.' Oh no! It means that I haven't got any food until tonight. Oh well, that will teach me, I think I'll go to the orchard after my swim to see what I can find there.

So, I had a leisurely swim and gave myself a good shake and off I trundled towards the orchard. On the way there I met with Dan the dog.

'Where are you off to then, Norman? You're a bit away from the farm, old son.'

I told him about missing breakfast and going to the orchard to see if I could find something that would tide me over until tonight's feed. 'Well, be careful, there are some strange goings-on in the area at the moment, that's why I'm checking up everywhere.'

'I will', I said, and waddled off down the lane once more.

Phut, phut, phut the noise was loud! I jumped onto the side of the lane remembering the last time the tractor came along. Here he comes puffing and wheezing. 'Hi!', I said, 'You still don't look too good mate, but I see you've got your tyre mended then. 'Aye', he said, 'but it's the old gear box mate, it's wearing out, but I think I can make it back to the yard.

'Okay, take it easy', I said and trundled on my way.

Just then I heard a strange noise, sort of grating or chewing, then up popped a head above the hedge on a tree branch. There sat a squirrel, chewing an acorn.

'Hi' he said, 'just having a spot of lunch'. My tummy began to rumble, 'Don't mention food', I said, 'I'm starving hungry.'

'Are you? Want a nut then?

'No thanks, I'm not a nut eater, I prefer something a bit softer.'

'Sorry I can't help you out. Happy hunting! With a swish of his tail he was off. It looked as though I was going to have to wait a bit longer.

Just then, a strange contraption came round the corner. It had big blades and a loud engine. Once again I jumped into the ditch for safety. 'Ouch!' I landed on something prickly. 'Hey' said a voice, 'what's going on?'

I had landed on Harry the hedgehog. 'I was just enjoying my lunch, thank you very much, now it's squashed.'

'Sorry' I said, gently rubbing where his prickles had spiked me.

'Have you got any spare lunch? Why, are you hungry mate? Am I hungry? Boy, am I hungry! Okay you can share. I've nearly had enough anyway. So I sat in the bottom of a ditch, sharing some lunch with a hedgehog. They will never believe me when I tell them in the farmyard, I thought.

'By the way, what was that big machine that went by a short time ago?'

'That', he said 'was a combine harvester.'

'A what?' I said, 'a combine harvester. It's used to cut the corn, etc. It comes every summer, haven't you seen it before?'

'No', I said 'perhaps it doesn't come to our farm, it's only a small farm you see.'

' Oh quite, you're right, they don't cut small farms, they need lots of room to turn round. I thought to myself, thank goodness, I would hate a great monster like that on our farm. Thank heaven for small mercies, as they say.

'I think I've had enough for one day, I'm off home now, bye Harry, see you.'
'Bye Norman, look after yourself old son, see you soon.'

'Yes mate, see you soon.'

THE MILK LORRY

'Hello', I said to the nearest girl (that's what I call the hens with whom I share) I mean that's where I sleep, in the chicken shed. 'Hi to you, dear boy. What have you planned for the day? Another adventure, if I know you.'

'No, no plans for today, I'm just going to take the day as it comes. See you later.'

Very wise, she looks at me with her head on one side as if to say, I believe you thousands wouldn't!

The morning looked like it was to be a mixture of rain and sun, so first of all a nice swim I think. Wheeeee! This is great, the water is really refreshing today. After I had had some fun chasing the frogs about in the water and some young newts too, I got out of the pond, had a little preen (put my feathers back into place) and set off towards the barn.

The barn is where my old tractor friend is. He comes out occasionally for a wash and polish, he is semi-retired now and only does little jobs around the farm, about which he is very pleased as he soon gets tired and has to stop to rest. A brand new tractor has taken over the ploughing, etc. he is quite friendly, but I don't know him as well as my old friend.

I got into the barn through the missing piece of board and there he stood, eyes closed, resting on his one good back wheel (the other three looked a little flat), as he was having forty winks (a little sleep to you and me).

'Oh hi Norman, what brings you here today? Well, I am at a bit of a loose end, so I thought I would come and see what's happening here for a change.

'What is happening here? Well, I say you would never believe what I have just heard from the milk lorry that came to collect the milk early this morning! It was like this you seeeeeeeeeee and he told me some news that made my feathers stand up on end!

'What!!!!!!!!!! No, I don't believe it, the farm is being sold? Never! What will we all do, where will all go? Are you sure you heard correctly? Well, I thought that's what he said, although there was a lot of noise going on. I'm going to do some checking fast, I thought to myself.

I said, 'See you later, with some better news I hope.'

I trundled out of the barn and went to find Dan the dog. He would know, I'm sure, I don't want to panic everyone until I'm sure of my facts!

I found Dan enjoying a nice juicy bone. 'Hi', I said, 'what's new mate? Any good news for us today?'

'Not a lot mate, except the milk lorry said (oh no, I thought, the worst news possible) that the Farmer is selling his milk himself from now on, some Organic Idea that the local people want him to bring in.'

I sat down with a bump. Phew, I thought, thank goodness for that! It shows how quickly the wrong information can get around.

'Oh,' I said meekly, 'that's a good idea.' And I went on my way back to the tractor before he could tell anyone else.

'Hi again,' I said. 'Our worries are over, my old mucker. You misheard the lorry with all the noise going on. The farmer is going sell his own MILK from now on, not the farm, I'm glad to say.'

'Oh! Sorry mate, I'll try and listen a bit more carefully next time, but thanks for coming and putting my mind at rest.'

I didn't tell him, but I was glad to hear the news, too.

BLACK RABBIT

All is quiet this morning, everyone has breakfasted, I've had a lovely swim and I'm now off to see my friend Dobbin to see how his friend Donk is. (He wasn't in the field last time I passed that way as he was having some new shoes fitted.)

As I trundled along the lane towards the field where they were, I met a black rabbit. I stared - a black rabbit - I wonder where he has come from?

'Morning', I said as we approached each other.

'Good morning', he said, 'although I don't know what's good about it, I'm lost! My owners left the cage open by mistake and I ventured out, thought I might just have a little look around and before I knew it I was lost!'

'Oh dear' I said, 'I might know someone who might be able to help you, or at least advise you what to do.'

I took him back to the farm, to where Roland and Rosie lived near the chicken house. He caused quite a stir with the chickens, they hadn't seen a black rabbit before. Come to think of it, neither had I. Anyway, I left him with the rabbits and the last I saw of them they were having a good old natter.

Back up the lane again I went to the field, and to my horror, no Dobbin and no Donk! Oh my goodness, what has happened to them? I ran up the lane as fast as I could towards the pond in the village to see if they had any news. Then past two more fields, when a familiar voice said over a farm gate, 'Hey, what's the hurry? No time to talk to two friends then?'

I looked up and there was Dobbin and Donk. I said, 'I was in a panic when you weren't in your usual field, I wondered what had happened to you.'

'Panic not, my dear friend, the farmer decided to move us up two fields to rest the other one as the grass was getting a bit short there. And I must say it makes a nice change as there are a few more trees for shade here, so we are well pleased.'

I chattered on for a few more minutes and then decided to return to the farm, to see if the black rabbit had sorted his problem out.

When I was walking back, I met the rabbit and Dan the dog walking towards the village. 'Hi' I said', 'Have you got yourself sorted? 'Yes,' said the rabbit . 'Dan here is going to take me back home, he thinks he knows the way as he knows the area quite well.'

'Oh good', I said and trundled on my way.

Dan walked with the rabbit and said, 'Well, my old china, I think this is where you came out and if I am not mistaken it is the bottom of your garden that I can see through the hedge. 'OOOOOOh lovely!' said the rabbit, 'Many thanks.'

'I'll just watch until you get near the house' said Dan, 'Just to make sure it is the right place.'

The rabbit approached the house and a little girl ran out.

She shouted 'Mummy, mummy, come quick! Richard is here, he is just hopping up the path', and she ran and put her arms around the rabbit and was so happy to see him. Dan watched until the mother came out and then he went back home to the farm.

Richard, well what a posh name, he thought, and what a lovely homecoming he had! What a lucky rabbit, he thought, in more ways than one! All's well that ends well. I wonder what tomorrow will bring? Hey ho, I'm off to have forty winks, it has been a tiring day.

CARNIVAL

Up early this morning, I plan to have a quick swim, then breakfast, and I am off to see my old friends Dobbin and Donk again.

There's a special Carnival going on in the village and they were going to be included. Dobbin is to pull one of the floats, whatever they are, and Donk is to give the youngest children rides. They were going to be 'poshed up' and I wanted to see what was going on, me being a nosy duck you know!

When I arrived at their field they weren't there, but I could hear noises coming from the barn that they slept in, so I waddled over. Well, what a surprise! There stood Dobbin, brass on his leather harness and shine! It almost dazzled me. 'My, my, you do look posh.'

'Wait until you see Donk then!' he replied. There stood Donk, a red plume on his head, red saddle and red reins. Well mate, if I didn't know better I would have thought it was Christmas! Where is your sack of parcels?'

'Huh!' said Donk 'You should be me, and don't call me 'mate' mate, unless you have something good to say.

'Sorry mate, only joking, you look very fine, the pair of you.'

At that moment they were being led out of the barn towards the village by a couple of people. One said to me, 'Hey duck, get back to the farmyard before you get lost.'

'Me, lost? No way', but I waddled off away from the unfriendly person and went on to the village. I don't think it was the best idea I had had as it turned out.

I called at the pond to see my friends and found out where the Carnival was being held. There were lots of people, tractors, cars and children by the dozen!

Before I could move, I was scooped into the air and put into a ring, people were staring at me and I was a bit worried. 10p to guess the name of the duck, 10p? What a cheek, I'm worth more than that! Well, I stayed there for a while and when they weren't looking, slipped away and hid under a tractor, phew, when a voice said, 'Hello my old mucker, it's me.' It was the old tractor, he had been brought out to be on show. He looked very smart, all polished up and that.

'Look,' he said 'I won a rosette, first prize too!'

'Oh, well done mate, you do look smart!'.

Just then two people came along and they were saying 'where has that duck gone, we need him for the winner.'

'Whattttttttt help, shhhhhhh said the old tractor, when they have gone, hop into my tool box they'll never find you there if you keep very quiet.'

I did as he said and remained there until the tractor went back home, which wasn't too long as he soon got tired.

Back in the barn, I was able to get out. 'Phew, thanks my old mucker. I think I will give the next Carnival a miss, not the sort of thing that's up my street.'

I went for a nice swim as I was hot and dusty after sitting in the tool box, but I was very thankful for being rescued. Tomorrow I will visit Dobbin and Donk to see how they got on, better than me, I hope.

Well, I'm off for forty winks now, tomorrow, well, who knows what tomorrow will bring!

WORK ON THE LOFT

Oh! yawn!!!. What a lovely sleep. What! Where is everyone? The chicken house was empty and very quiet. I scrambled out of my bed and went outside. There were the hens all chattering, cleaning themselves after their breakfast.

'Why didn't you wake me?' I said.

'Well, my boy, you looked so peaceful and in such a deep sleep we thought we would let you sleep in this morning. Don't worry they have saved some breakfast for you.'

'Phew, thanks,' I said, relieved that I hadn't missed out. I was feeling very hungry.

After I had finished, I had a rest at the side of the pond until I thought I was ready to have my morning dip. You see, I usually had it first, then breakfast afterwards, but I did it in reverse this morning.

What to do today? I spent extra time in the pond and when I finally came out it was to find Dan the dog waiting for me to let me know that the two mice Maurice and Mindy who lived in the loft in the big barn wanted to see me.

'Okay,' I said, 'I'll go now before I begin anything else.'

I waddled up to the barn and a voice said to me, 'Morning Norman!'

It was Charlie, one of the cats, 'What are you doing over this side of the farm?' 'Coming to see us,' said a second voice. It was Cindy, the other cat.

'No,' I said, 'not at the moment, why, do you have a problem?'

'Nooooooo,' they said 'just nosy, that's all.'

I was very careful not to let them know that I was visiting the mice, because, although the cats appeared friendly, they could also tease and frighten the mice sometimes.

I said in a loud voice, 'I came to see my old friend Tractor as a matter of fact,' which was true in a way, as I always had a word when I came to the big barn especially now he didn't get out so much. He was glad of a natter now and then.

The cats followed me into the barn and sat down for a wash. I went to Tractor and said, 'Morning me old mate, how are you today?' The tractor noticed my raised eyebrows and looked at the cats. He understood what was going on.

'Good to see you,' and we chatted on until the cats got bored and paddled off to their favourite spot on the shed roof. Once they were out of earshot I told Tractor why I was really here although I told him 'I wanted to see you too, mate.' After a while I flew up to see what the two mice wanted. They were worried as they had overheard the Farmer talking and he said that the loft was going to be cleared as there were some repairs that needed doing. 'Which leaves us homeless!' they said, 'At least, for a while.' 'Don't worry,' I said, 'I will have a word with my ladies (the chickens) and we will see what we can come up with.' I told Tractor what was going on and he said he would help if he could.

I found most of the hens resting as it was close to midday.

'Well,' said one of the hens, 'give us a little time to think it over and we will see what we can up with, we won't be long.'

I wandered off, not wanting to worry them too much, as this was important because whatever they came up with could affect the mice a great deal.

A hen wandered up to me not wanting to make a big issue of it, as the cats were on the prowl and they didn't want to let them get wind of things.

'We have decided that, if it is only short term, they can move in with us. We have a spare corner that will be safe for them, as long as they know that it is only short term.'

'Great,' I said, 'I'll mosey over and let them know.'

I found the mice busy packing up their belongings and told them what the plan was. Dan would keep the cats busy, the hens would post lookouts and I would be on hand to create a diversion if necessary. It was late afternoon whilst the cats were snoozing that we put the plan into action. Dan lay down nearby with one eye open making out he was snoozing too. The hens took up their positions, which took a little while, as they tried to act as naturally as they could, and I nestled down in some dust to have a dust bath. It went like clockwork and the mice were safely installed.

'Thanks,' they said, 'please thank everyone for us as without their help we could not have managed it.'

I passed on the message and everyone relaxed once more. Just in time too, as the cats were stretching after their afternoon snooze, phew!

BABY RABBIT

As I walked along the farmyard, I saw someone hiding in the bushes which lined the path to the kitchen garden. It was Roland, one of the rabbits which lived under the chicken house.

'What's up?' I asked in a quiet voice, so as not to frighten him.

'One of the youngest children has wandered off!' he said, 'and I am quietly looking for him as he is the smallest one and has no sense of direction, I'm afraid.

'Right!' I said, I will put the word out and everyone will search their part of the farmyard and Dan will do the outer area of the farm. Try not to worry.'

Soon the word had gone around and the yard was busy with everyone searching out the corners that weren't usually used. After a very thorough search for him, no trace was found. Two very worried parents were looking sad.

'Don't worry,' I said, 'I'll have a fly around' (I am still not very keen on flying) 'to see if I can spot anything from the air.'

I took off and very carefully flew back and forth across the farm, then widened my search and low and behold, I spotted him! He had hopped into the kitchen garden and was merrily feeding on some young cabbages. I landed quite a way away from him, so as not to frighten him, and casually walked up to him.

'Hello, I'm Norman, what's your name?'

'I'm Cedric,' he said.

'I think your mum is looking for you, she wants to show you how to find some of the sweetest grass and other things.

'But it's lovely here' he said, 'and lots to eat too!'

'Yes, I know,' I said, 'but this is the farmer's kitchen garden and he won't be very pleased to see you here! I think you should come with me, see your mum and let her know that you are safe. Then you can carry on playing with your brothers and sisters until dinner time.

'Oh, okay, I suppose I should have said where I was going.'

We trundled back to the farmyard, which as it turned out wasn't too far, and his mum Rosie was so pleased to see him safe that she didn't scold him too much.

Everyone was relieved to see him back and the farmyard settled down once more, all's well that ends well, thank goodness!